This book
belongs to

Eva ♡

....

Cuddle's Fan Pages

Here's what other children have to say about their favourite kitten and her latest adventure!

"I really like this magical book. My favourite part is when the girls meet Cosmo: it's really exciting! I didn't think anything could be as cute as my new kittens, but Cuddle comes awfully close!" Carmen, age 7

"I didn't like the troll being nasty to Cosmo – I was glad Cuddle, Olivia and Grace were there to help. Cuddle is my favourite character because she persuaded Cosmo to never give up, and I liked it when she jumped on Mossfly's foot." Isabel, age 7

"This is the best book of the series. I love Cosmo the unicorn and am so glad Cuddle helped him make friends he could laugh with." Megan, age 8

"My favourite part was when the troll stuck his two fingers in his ears because it nearly made me laugh my head off." Piper, age 7

"I enjoyed this book so much. I wish I could travel with Cuddle, Olivia and Grace to Miss Rosamund's School for Magical Creatures. I would love to learn some magic spells to try out at school." Izzy, age 7

"Olivia and Grace are lovely, kind friends who include Cosmo the unicorn. I stayed up late to read the whole book because it was brilliant!" Hattie, age 6

"I like this story because I love unicorns. I wish I could go to a magical school. It made me laugh when Cuddle leapt at Miss Rosamund's feet to introduce herself." Emily, age 8

Cuddle
★ the cutest kitten ★

School of Spells

Other books about
Cuddle the Cutest Kitten:

Magical Friends
Superstar Dreams
Princess Party Sleepover

Cuddle

★ the cutest kitten ★

School of Spells

by Hayley Daze
illustrated by Ann Kronheimer
cover illustrated by Amanda Gulliver

A catalogue record for this book is available from the British Library

Published by Ladybird Books Ltd
A Penguin Company
Penguin Books Ltd., 80 Strand, London WC2R 0RL, UK
Penguin Books Australia Ltd., Camberwell, Victoria, Australia
Penguin Group (NZ) 67 Apollo Drive, Rosedale,
North Shore 0632, New Zealand

001 – 1 3 5 7 9 10 8 6 4 2
Series created by Working Partners Limited, London WC1X 9HH
Text © Working Partners Ltd MMXI
Cover illustration © Working Partners Ltd MMXI
Interior illustrations © Ladybird Books Ltd MMXI

Special thanks to Elizabeth Galloway

ISBN: 978-1-40930-853-9
Printed in England

Mixed Sources

Product group from well-managed
forests and other controlled sources
www.fsc.org   Cert no. SA-COC-001592
© 1996 Forest Stewardship Council

FSC

For Emily and Jessica Cowlard and Lottie Perryman –
wishing you all many magical adventures

Cuddle the kitten has black-and-white fur,
A cute crooked tail, and a very loud purr.
Her two best friends, Olivia and Grace,
Know Cuddle's world is a special place!

Just give her a cuddle, then everything spins;
A twitch of her whiskers, and magic begins!
So if you see a sunbeam, and hear Cuddle's bell,
You can join in the adventures as well!

Contents

Chapter One
Fairy Fun

Olivia squeezed her eyes shut. "Abracadabra, fiddle-de-dee, show me my wand, as fast as can be!" She opened them again and looked at the dressing-up box on the lawn of her back garden. A pirate hat and a pink feather boa were spilling out of it, but Olivia sighed. "I can't see my wand anywhere," she said to Grace.

The two girls were in fancy dress. Olivia's fairy outfit was a purple leotard and tutu and pink net wings covered in silver sparkle.

Her mum had made the outfit for Olivia on her sewing machine. Slung over her shoulder was the little bag

she took everywhere. Grace was dressed up as an elf, in green shorts and T-shirt, and pointy plastic ears hooked over her real ones.

"Don't worry," Grace said. "My mum says I'm good at finding things. When we lived on a farm, I used to look for where the chickens had laid their eggs. I'll help you find your wand."

It was a grey day in Catterton, with clouds squatting low over the houses and blocks of flats. Olivia and

Grace had decided to brighten up the garden, turning it into a fairy grotto. Olivia had strung daisy chains from the branches of the trees, while Grace had lined up her mum's garden gnome collection on top of the fence.

The girls knelt beside the pot plants on the patio, searching among the leaves and flowers.

"If only I was a proper fairy," Olivia said. "Then I could use magic to find it."

Grace jumped up, her eyes shining. "We do know someone with real magic."

"Cuddle!" Olivia cried.

The girls grinned at each other. Cuddle was a cute kitten who took them on amazing magical adventures.

Just then, a beam of sunlight reached through the clouds It shimmered in the air like a golden rainbow, shining right on to the dressing-up box.

Jingle jangle jingle jangle jingle.

"That's Cuddle's bell!" Grace cried. "She's here!"

The girls ran towards the dressing-up box and looked inside. Its contents quivered, and a black-and-white tail with a kink in its tip poked through. Then came a pair of black paws, and finally a furry white face.

"Cuddle!" Olivia exclaimed. "And look what she's found!"

The kitten had a purple plastic wand in her mouth. Olivia tucked it inside her bag. "Clever Cuddle," Grace said, and tickled the kitten under the chin, just where her purr was rumbling. With a mew, Cuddle sprang into Grace's arms, the silver bell on her pink collar jangling.

Both girls shut their eyes as the kitten's purr made their skin tingle all over.

"I feel like I'm covered in fizzy sherbet," Olivia murmured. "I

wonder where Cuddle will take us
this time . . ."

***

Olivia rubbed her eyes. The girls were
standing on a large stretch of grass.
White stripes marked out a pitch and
on the edge of the playing field was
what looked like a school building
with iron gates and lots of little
windows winking in the sunlight.

Olivia could hear chattering and shouts of laughter coming from a playground to the side of the building.

"Why would Cuddle bring us to a school?" she said to Grace. "We go to one of these all the time."

The kitten jumped down from Grace's arms and scampered across the grass towards the cries of other children. But as the girls stepped inside the playground, they gasped with amazement.

"These aren't children!" Grace cried, gazing around her. The two of them turned in a slow circle, their eyes wide as they took everything in.

"Wheeeee!" shouted a pixie, kicking with his curly-toed shoes as he whizzed down a slide. He jumped off the end, and Olivia could see that he only came up to her waist.

A group of elves, dressed in green like Grace, were playing football with a small ball against a team of gnomes.

"Goal!" yelled one of the elves. "Good shot!"

"I don't believe it," Olivia whispered. "Look!" She pointed into the air and Cuddle mewed with excitement.

Three fairies flew over their heads, pausing to flutter around a tall sign. As they passed over, glitter fell down over the girls' shoulders.

Olivia shook the glitter from her hair and laughed.

Gazing back up at the sign, she saw golden letters painted on it. "Miss Rosamund's School for Magical Creatures," she read out loud.

Olivia turned to Grace, her eyes bright. "We're at a school for magic!"

Chapter Two
The Shy Unicorn

"Come on," Grace said. "Let's ask if we can play, too!" They ran to join the creatures, Cuddle skipping beside them. Grace gazed up at the fairies playing above them.

"Your wings look just like theirs," she said to Olivia.

"Hello!" one of the fairies called down. "Have you come to join Miss

Rosamund's school?"

"We hope so!" Grace called back.
Cuddle swerved to the left, bounding
towards a broad tree at the edge of the
playing field. It was covered in pink,
yellow and blue flowers.

A white pony stood underneath
it, munching. Sticking out from his
forehead was a long horn, twisted
into a spiral like a seashell. It had a

kink in its tip, just like Cuddle's tail.
Grace's mouth dropped open.
"Look – a unicorn!"

At the sound of her voice, the unicorn's cheeks went rosy pink. He dropped his flowers and ducked behind the trunk, out of sight.

"I think he's shy," Olivia whispered.

Cuddle peered round the trunk, stretching her pink nose into the air.

"What's she doing?" Grace wondered.

The unicorn's long white muzzle poked out. He leaned down and gently touched his nose to Cuddle's.

She mewed and jumped on to his back, curling up just behind his head.

"She's making friends," Olivia said, clapping her hands.

Cuddle's tail brushed against the unicorn's neck. "Neigh-heehee!" he snorted, and shook as if she were tickling him. He trotted round the tree trunk, picking his hooves up high. Cuddle gave a mew as she bounced on his back.

"Wow," Grace said. "It's almost like he's dancing!"

The unicorn stopped dancing and his eyelashes fluttered. "Thank you," he said.

"You can talk!" Olivia gasped. "Please don't be scared of us. I'm Olivia. This is Grace, and you've met Cuddle, our kitten."

"I'm Cosmo," the unicorn said quietly.

"Nice to meet you, Cosmo," Grace said. "Why don't we go and play, too?"

"Because no one wants to play with a silly unicorn," a voice said.

The girls looked round. Standing beside them was a troll. His skin was

as green and warty as a toad's, and he
had yellow eyes. The troll jammed his
thumbs into his ears and waggled his
fingers. "Stupid putrid Cosmo!" he
jeered.

Olivia put her hands on her hips.
"Stop it! Calling people names is
nasty." The troll stuck his tongue out
and sloped off.

Grace patted Cosmo's silky mane. "Let's go and play."

But Cosmo hung his head and sighed.

Olivia took Grace's hand, pulling her aside. "I think he's too shy to join in," she said. "And that troll's making him feel even worse."

"That must be why Cuddle's brought us here," Grace whispered. "To help Cosmo make friends!"

Chapter Three
Miss Rosamund
Arrives

Tinkle tinkle tinkle.

"What's that?" Grace asked.

"It's Miss Rosamund," Cosmo said. "She's our head teacher."

Tinkle tinkle tinkle.

Puff! A plump lady with silver hair appeared in an explosion of glitter. She was wearing a pink gown, and in one hand she had a silver wand with

a star on top. In the other, she held a
silver bell.

Miss Rosamund tinkled the bell
again. "Time for lessons!" she called,
her cheeks dimpling as she smiled.

"Come on, everyone! You're all
going to learn your own special
magic today."

Olivia gasped. "Well, that beats
learning times tables!"

Miss Rosamund walked into
the school building, the magical
creatures skipping along behind her.

Cuddle flicked her crooked tail and ran through the open doorway to join them. "Good idea, Cuddle," Grace said. "We can learn about magic too. Come on, Cosmo!"

They hurried after the little kitten. But then the troll crawled out from under the slide.

"Looking forward to the magic lessons?" he asked Cosmo.

"Yes," Cosmo replied, backing away.

"Why?" the troll demanded. "Silly unicorns can't do magic. Everyone's going to laugh at you!"

"Hey," Grace said. "We've already told you to stop being mean."

"*Pfffffft!*" The troll made a loud raspberry sound and stomped after the other creatures.

"Just ignore him, Cosmo," Olivia said.

But the unicorn was already trotting back towards the tree, his head drooping.

Grace scooped up Cuddle and the girls ran to join him.

"Please come to the lesson," Grace said. "You might make some new friends."

Tears glittered like jewels on Cosmo's long eyelashes. "But I can't do magic. Why would anyone want to be friends with a unicorn who can't cast spells?"

Chapter Four
Whizzing Wands

"Miaow!" Cuddle wiggled her whiskers.

The branches above them rustled, and hundreds of pink, yellow and blue petals showered down. They caught in Cosmo's mane and Olivia's fairy wings, and stuck on to Grace's pointy ears.

Cuddle flicked one off her nose

with her pink tongue.

Cosmo's eyes were wide. "Did
Cuddle make this happen?" he asked.

Grace nodded. "She's a magical
kitten. If a little kitten like Cuddle can
make magic, I'm sure a unicorn can
too! She wants to help you, Cosmo –
and so do we. Please go to the magic
lesson!"

"All right," he agreed. "But only if you and Olivia come too."

Grace threw her arms round Cosmo's long neck. "Of course we will!"

Olivia glanced towards the school door, where the other students had

followed Miss Rosamund. "And we'd better hurry," she added, "or we'll be late for the lesson."

Cosmo knelt down on the lawn, folding his legs beneath him.

"All aboard the Cosmo Express!"

Grace gently held on to Cosmo's

mane and pulled herself up on his back. She'd ridden lots of ponies before, but never a unicorn!

Olivia sat behind, her arms around Grace's waist. Cuddle sprang into Grace's lap.

Cosmo stood up and galloped towards the school building.

He skipped from hoof to hoof, his tail swishing along to the rhythm of his steps.

"Woo-hoo!" Grace cheered. "This is an amazing galloping dance, Cosmo!"

As they approached the school door, he ducked his head beneath the door frame and trotted down the corridor, his hooves clip-clopping.

The girls gasped as each floor tile lit up red, yellow or blue as Cosmo stepped over it. "It's magic!" Grace cried.

Cosmo gave a gentle neigh. "Of course it is. We're in a magic school, remember?"

They arrived outside a classroom and the girls slid from Cosmo's back. Then they followed him inside.

Grace sank on to a plump cushion beside the other elves, gnomes and fairies who were arranged in a circle round Miss Rosamund. Olivia sat beside her on a purple velvet cushion. On the shelves around the classroom were little cauldrons,

glass jars stuffed full of odd-looking
ingredients and piles of glitter dust.

"I've never been in a classroom
like this before," Grace whispered to
Olivia.

"Hello, Cosmo," Miss Rosamund said. "I see you've brought two new pupils."

Cosmo knelt down beside the girls. Cuddle leapt from his back, landing at Miss Rosamund's feet.

"And who have we here?" she asked.

"That's Cuddle," Olivia explained. "I'm Olivia, and this is Grace."

"Welcome to you all," Miss Rosamund said. "I usually ring my bell to show that the lesson has started, but maybe Cuddle could ring hers today."

The little kitten shook her head, making her bell jingle. The magical creatures giggled, and Cuddle hopped on to Olivia's knee. Cosmo stood beside Grace.

Miss Rosamund waved her silver wand, and to the girls' amazement, wooden bookcases appeared beneath the shelves. Even though they were crammed with books, they hovered above the floor.

Olivia's eyes darted over their spines. "*Flying for Beginners, 101 Tricks to Play on Humans, Magic Made Easy,*" she read in a whisper. "They're all about magic!"

Miss Rosamund walked over to a large desk at one end of the classroom. On it was a pen pot filled with strange-looking sticks. Miss Rosamund stood behind the desk and, holding her wand like a pencil,

wrote pink letters in the air: "MY
MAGICAL GIFT".

"Wow," Grace murmured. "It's like
a magical whiteboard."

"Now, class," Miss Rosamund said.
"Everyone has their own special kind
of magic, and today you're going to
find yours."

"But how will we know when we've

found it?" a pixie
asked, scratching
his head.

Miss Rosamund
smiled. "You'll
know," she said.
"Your tummy will tingle, and you'll
feel so happy, you could float up into
the clouds. I found my special magic
when I was trying to cast a spell to
make lemonade. Instead, I magicked
a special teacher's cloak." She stroked
the pink silk of her cloak, smiling.
"That's how I knew I was meant to set
up a school for magic!"

She waved her wand once more and
the sticks floated out of the pen pot.

They were a rainbow of colours, each with a different shape at the top.

"Magic wands!" Olivia said, swinging her legs.

Miss Rosamund raised her wand. "Magic wands, hear my call, find your owner, one and all!"

With a whoosh, the wands whizzed over everyone's heads, like a fireworks display.

Cuddle leapt on to Olivia's shoulder, and as a red wand with a heart at its tip zoomed past, she sprang up and caught it between her teeth.

She jumped to the ground to give it to Cosmo.

"Look, everyone else is getting their own wand too," Grace said.

A gnome cheered as he caught a green wand with a flower at the top, while a wand with a diamond shape landed in a giggling pixie's hand.

Olivia opened her bag and took out
her plastic wand. "You never know,"
she said to Grace, "we might need one
too."

Miss Rosamund clapped her hands
and the class turned to look at her.

"Here comes the fun part," she said,
her eyes twinkling. "First, I want you
to split up into groups. Then each

group must work together to practise your very own magic spells. Off you go!"

The creatures jumped off their cushions and rushed to join up.

The gnomes immediately stood together, and so did the pixies. The elves gathered by one of the bookcases.

Cosmo's cheeks reddened and he lowered his gaze to the floor.

"Oh no," Grace whispered. "The other pupils aren't mixing up at all."

"And Cosmo's the only unicorn," Olivia said. "He's going to be left out!"

Chapter Five
Mean Mossfly

Olivia ran over to the three fairies,
who were fluttering beside Miss
Rosamund's desk. "Would you like
to be in a group with me and my
friends?" she asked.

The fairies glanced at each other
and gave a small nod. "Okay, we'll be
in your group," one of them said.

Olivia led them over to Cosmo.

Grace was hurrying back too, leading an elf by the hand.

"This is Hal," Grace said. "His ears are even pointier than mine."

One of the fairies said, "We're Dilly, Milly and Tilly."

"Miaow!" Cuddle trotted up to them. She was followed by a gnome in a red hat.

"And I'm Norris," the gnome said.

The girls introduced themselves, then Grace gently nudged Cosmo forward. "Go on," she whispered in his ear.

"I'm Cosmo," he said very quietly.

"Well done," Olivia whispered. Aloud, she said, "Our group's ready to start now."

"Not quite," a sneering voice said. It was the troll.

The fairy called Dilly folded her arms. "What do you want, Mossy?"

"My name's Mossfly," the troll said crossly. "I'm going to be in your group too. I can't wait to see the useless unicorn mess this – eek!"

Cuddle had pounced on his foot. He waved it about, trying to shake her away.

"Get off me!" Mossfly shouted. Grace carefully peeled Cuddle away from the troll. "No wonder our kitten doesn't like you," she said. "You're being mean. You can be in our group, but only if you're nice to everyone."

Mossfly scowled, but eventually he nodded.

"Who wants to go first?" Olivia asked, sitting back down on one of the cushions. Cuddle curled up beside her.

"Me!" Hal the elf cried. He took an acorn out of his pocket. "I found this near the tree,"  he explained. He held out his wand, which had a leaf shape on the end, screwed his eyes shut, and chanted, "Huffle, puffle, float to the moon, make this acorn a blue balloon!"

With a puff, the acorn transformed into a shiny blue balloon with a long ribbon knotted to it. Hal beamed as he held it. Grace whistled in approval, while Olivia clapped.

"You've found your gift!" Miss Rosumund cried, walking over.

"Well done, Hal. You're clearly meant
to work with nature."

"I'll go next," Norris the gnome
said. He rubbed his tummy with one
hand and waved his wand with the
other.

The sweetie shape at the end
flashed in the sunshine. Norris said,
"Hizzle, fizzle, nice ice cream, make
the biggest bowl I've ever seen!"

But no ice cream appeared. Instead,

Norris's red hat turned green. Mossfly put his warty hands over his mouth as if he were trying not to laugh.

Miss Rosumund bent down. "I think your magic gift is colours, not food," she whispered in Norris's ear.

"Norris has given us an idea," Milly said. The three fairies held their wands together so the moon shapes at the end were touching.

Together they chanted, "Sugar, icing, chocolate flakes, conjure a plate of delicious cakes!"

Golden sparks fizzed from their wands and a plate of floating cakes appeared in the air. They were in paper cases and coated with pink icing.

"Fairy cakes!" Grace said. "Yummy! So food is your magic gift!"

"Who wants icky pink?" Mossfly said. He pointed his spider-tipped wand at the plate, and yelled, "Mud and worms, slugs and grime, cover those nasty cakes in slime!"

With a flash, oozing green slime appeared on the cakes, dripping off them like pond weed.

"Oh no!" the fairies cried.

"Miaow!" Cuddle stared up at Mossfly, her whiskers twitching. The slime disappeared in a cloud of green smoke.

The fairies clapped. "Thank you, Cuddle!" they said in their tinkling voices.

"It's your turn now," Olivia said to Cosmo. The unicorn stared at the group. His eyes were wide and his knees trembled.

Cosmo shook his head from side to side, waving his wand.

"That's it!" Grace said. But the wand slipped out from between the unicorn's teeth and plopped on to one of the cushions.

"It's no good," Cosmo said. "I don't have a magical gift." Then he turned and raced out of the classroom.

"Cosmo, come back!" Grace and Olivia cried. Had Cosmo given up on magic school for good?

Chapter Six
Try, Try, Try Again

Cuddle ran out into the corridor after the unicorn. All Grace and Olivia could hear were soft mews from Cuddle and Cosmo's neighs.

"It's almost as though they're talking to each other," Olivia said.

Grace shrugged. "Perhaps they are."

Then a cloud of silver glitter billowed into the classroom, followed by Cuddle riding on Cosmo's back.

Olivia patted Cosmo's long neck.

"I'm so glad you're back. Remember what Miss Rosamund said – we've all got a magical gift. Please try!"

"Please, Cosmo!" the three fairies begged.

"Have a go!" Hal said, waving his balloon.

"You're right," Cosmo said. "I shouldn't give up."

Cosmo lowered his head to pick up the wand, and Cuddle leapt back down to the floor. She batted Cosmo's horn gently with her paw.

"Oh," Cosmo said, nodding at the little kitten. "Cuddle's just given me an idea. I can't pick up my wand properly. I'm going to try using my horn as a wand instead."

Cosmo waved his white horn as if he were casting a spell, but nothing happened. "I still can't do it," he murmured.

Cuddle rubbed against Cosmo's front legs.

Then she hopped from paw to paw, her ears flicking and her tail swishing.

"She's dancing," Grace murmured to Olivia. "Hey! If we can get Cosmo to dance, maybe he'll stop being so nervous and his spell will work."

"Good idea," Olivia agreed.

She took Grace's hand, and the girls danced round Cuddle, skipping and twirling.

"That looks fun!" Norris said.

He hooked his arm through Hal's and they followed Grace, Olivia and Cuddle.

The three fairies fluttered after them, dancing on the tips of their toes like ballerinas. Even Mossfly joined in, jumping and waving his arms above his head.

Cuddle led them around the cushions and in between the floating bookcases.

"Come on, Cosmo!" Olivia called. "You're the best dancer of all!"

The unicorn's white brow furrowed, but then he galloped after the line of dancers. His four legs were a blur as he hopped and twirled.

Grace gasped. "Look at Cosmo's horn!" she said to Olivia. It had burst into a rainbow of colours.

As he danced, Cosmo waved his horn and chanted: "I love to eat flowers and watch clouds in the skies, but in laughter and friendship true happiness lies!"

All the dancers stopped still. Grace squeezed Olivia's hand. Would Cosmo's spell work?

Chapter Seven
The Gift of Friendship

"Hee hee hee," giggled Tilly the fairy.

"Ha ha ha!" chuckled Hal the elf.

"HO HO HO!" Norris the gnome bellowed.

Grace glanced at Olivia. "Are they laughing at Cosmo?" she whispered.

But Olivia's shoulders trembled. She was giggling too!

She pointed to Cosmo. The
unicorn's ears quivered as he tossed
his head back, giving a great snort of
laughter.

"Cosmo's spell worked," Olivia
said, in between chuckles.

Mossfly was still scowling. But
then his shoulders started to shake
and his belly jiggled. "Ha! Hee!"

he chortled. He threw himself to the
ground, thumping it with his fist.
"A-hoo-hoo!"

Grace giggled. "The spell's even
worked on Mossfly!"

All the other groups and Miss
Rosamund hurried over.

"What's going on?" asked a pixie.
"Did someone make a joke?"

Miss Rosamund's eyes twinkled.
"Perhaps Cosmo can explain."

The unicorn's crooked horn shimmered with colour. He coughed, clearing his throat, then spoke in the loudest voice the girls had heard him use. "My tummy tingles and I think I could float up into the sky," he said. "I must have found my magical gift, Miss Rosamund. It's making people laugh."

"That's wonderful news!" Miss Rosamund cried.

She hurried over to her desk, where "MY MAGICAL GIFT" still hung in pink letters in the air. Holding her wand as a pencil once more, she wrote underneath, 'Cosmo's spell: gold star'.

Then she waved her wand again and

a golden star appeared beside the words. Cosmo's blue eyes widened. "I've never had a gold star before!"

Cosmo's spell: q

"I think Cuddle deserves a star as well," Miss Rosamund said with a smile.

"Miaow!" Cuddle hopped across to Miss Rosamund, jumping into her arms. She held the little kitten in the

crook of her plump arm, stroking the
white fur on Cuddle's tummy.

"You really are the cutest kitten,"
Miss Rosamund said. She waved her
wand, and a tiny silver star appeared
on Cuddle's collar, dangling next to
her bell. "There's a star for you, too,
for all your help today."

Mossfly stepped in front of the

girls and the unicorn.

"Er, Cosmo," the troll began. He was tapping the spidery tip of his wand against his palm, as if he were nervous. "I'm sorry I called you those names," he said. "I'm going to try to be nicer from now on."

"That's all right, Mossfly," Cosmo replied.

Olivia handed the troll her plastic purple wand. "I think it suits you better than that horrible spider wand," she said.

Mossfly gave a lopsided grin.

He sat on one
of the cushions,
waving his new
wand.

"It's not like
we need wands
anyway," Olivia
said with a sigh. "We can't do magic."

"Oh yes, you can," Miss Rosamund
said, stepping beside them. Cuddle
was still in her arms, pink sparkles
shimmering round both of them.
She nodded towards Cosmo. "Just
look at him."

The unicorn was surrounded by
the other magical creatures, his horn
shining with colour.

"What do you call a unicorn without a horn?" Cosmo asked Hal the elf. "A u-no-horn!"

Hal doubled up with laughter, almost letting go of his balloon.

Miss Rosamund smiled at the girls. "Before Cosmo met you and Cuddle, he was shy and lonely. You've made him happy," she said. "You two have the greatest magical gift of all – the gift of friendship."

Chapter Eight
Butterfly Brooches

"Miaow!" Cuddle scrambled out of Miss Rosamund's arms. She nuzzled against Olivia's ankles, her fur tickling her bare skin, then wound around Grace's legs.

"It's time for Cuddle to take us home," Grace said to Miss Rosamund.

Cosmo trotted over to them, one of the fairies perched on his back.

"Before you go, I'd like to do one last magic trick."

"What's that?" Olivia asked.

Cosmo swirled his horn in the air. "Hold hands around me," he said.

Grace, Olivia, Norris, Hal and all the fairies held hands, with the fairies dipping and hovering in the air.

"Now start dancing," Cosmo said. As he stood in the centre of the circle, Grace and Olivia skipped round and round with all the others.

Cosmo waved his horn and it burst into colour. "Little girls and kitten too, here's a gift from us to you." He gave a final swirl of his horn and a shower of silk butterflies drifted down from the air. Olivia and Grace cried out and held out their hands to catch one.

On the back of each silk butterfly was a little pin. Grace pinned her butterfly brooch to her green jumper and Olivia attached hers to her leotard.

"Now you have something to remember us by," Cosmo explained.

Grace and Olivia each gave him a kiss on his soft velvety nose.

"Thank you, Cosmo!" they chorused.

The fairies blew kisses to the girls, and Norris and Hal waved their hats in the air. Even Mossfly stuck his fingers in his mouth and blew a goodbye whistle.

"Farewell!" Miss Rosamund called.

"Never forget your special gift!"

The creatures, the classroom and the floating bookcases were already becoming blurred. The girls tingled all over as the magical school faded away...

Olivia opened her eyes. She was curled up inside something small and dark. Grace was squashed next to her, and she could feel Cuddle's whiskers brushing against her arm.

She reached up, finding the edge of the container, and pulled herself upright.

"We're inside the dressing-up box in my garden!" Olivia said.

She climbed out of the box. Grace swung her legs over the side and jumped out too.

"Look! We're still wearing our brooches," Olivia gasped. She stroked the silk butterfly on her leotard and Grace smiled as she peered down at her own brooch.

There was a rustling noise inside the box and Cuddle jumped out, landing on Grace's feet.

She had a pink feather boa wound round her neck.

"Cuddle's a real glamour-puss," Olivia said, stroking the kitten's silky ears. Cuddle touched her nose to Olivia's fingers and then to Grace's. Then she ran towards a rose bush and disappeared in a puff of sparkles.

"See you soon, Cuddle!" Olivia called after her.

Grace turned to Olivia. "My tummy's tingling and I feel like floating into the sky," she said. "I think I know what's even more magical than a fairy or an elf!"

Olivia looked puzzled. "What?"

"Being friends!"

Grace pulled a pirate hat out of the dressing-up box and put it on her head. Olivia laughed and put her arm through Grace's.

The two girls skipped up the garden path towards the kitchen door. Olivia pushed it open. "Who needs wands?" she said. "We can make our own magic every day!"

If you love Cuddle the Cutest Kitten,
then why not try the
Puddle the Naughtiest Puppy stories?
Read on for a sneak peek at
Puddle's very first adventure,
MAGIC CARPET RIDE...

Magic Carpet Ride

Ruby hopscotched down Grandad's garden path, splashing her way through the puddles. Her wellies sent water spraying high into the air. Dots of mud splattered her dress. Ruby loved how the raindrops caught in her plaits.

"The crowd goes wild," Ruby yelled as she hopped, skipped and jumped towards an imaginary finish line. "Ruby, the World Champion Puddle Jumper, wins again!"

Ruby raised her arms in victory, but just as she reached the last puddle, a puppy splashed right into the middle of it, soaking her.

"Hello!" Ruby said, smiling and wringing out her plaits. "Where did you come from?" She leaned down to check the puppy's neck for a collar, but he didn't have one. "Are you lost?"

The puppy shook his head. Raindrops flew from his floppy ears.

"Would you like to play with my cousin Harry and me?" Ruby asked.

The puppy raced Ruby up the

garden path. They burst through the front door of Grandad's cottage and into the lounge.

Harry was sitting in the window seat, reading his puzzle book. He looked up and pushed back his glasses, which had slipped down his nose. "I don't think puppies are allowed in the house," he said, looking worried. "Especially not wet puppies with muddy paws!"

The puppy bounced around the room, knocking over Harry's pile of library books and Grandad's umbrella stand. He ran up to Harry and snatched the puzzle book right out of his hands.

"Hey, you give that back," Harry called, but he was grinning. "You're not just muddy, are you? You're a naughty puppy!"

The puppy dropped the book and dashed back outside, with Ruby close behind. The rain was falling heavily now. One of the raindrops landed with a plop on the tip of Ruby's nose. Others slid down her cheek, her dress and even the toes of her wellies.

"Come on, Harry," Ruby called. She watched him pull on his wellies and peer into the garden.

"It's too muddy to play outside," Harry said, looking down at his nice white shirt and his pressed beige trousers.

The puppy ran towards Harry, splashing through the puddles, and jumped up to his chest. Harry nearly fell over.

"Urgh!" groaned Harry, wiping mud from his shirt. "I don't think I've ever been this filthy in my life." But he was smiling happily, and he bent to stroke the puppy's soggy ears.

"I think he likes you," Ruby said. "I wonder what his name is."

"We should call him Puddle," Harry said. "He splashes in enough of them."

"Would you like that name, boy?"

asked Ruby.

The puppy offered her a muddy paw.

"That's a deal, then. Puddle it is," Ruby said, shaking his paw.

She and the puppy splashed in every puddle on the path, Ruby's pigtails bouncing up and down.

"Come on, Harry, try this. It's great!"

Harry wiped specks of muddy water from his glasses. "I don't think so," he said.

Puddle barked and danced circles round a big puddle. Ruby skipped over, splashing water into the air as she went.

The puppy looked from Ruby to Harry.

"Stop him," Harry groaned. "He's going to jump."

But the puppy leapt into the puddle and . . .

Ruby gasped and looked at Harry. His eyes were wide as he stared at the puddle.

"The naughty puppy's disappeared!" they said together.

***

To read more about Puddle the Naughtiest Puppy, get your copy of MAGIC CARPET RIDE Out now!

Cuddle
★ the cutest kitten ★

Magical Friends

Meet Olivia, Grace and Cuddle in their first adventure!

New friends Olivia and Grace are amazed when cute kitten Cuddle appears and whisks them away to an ancient Egyptian pyramid. Can they help Beset find the Pharaoh's kitten inside it?

Find out in MAGICAL FRIENDS...

Cuddle

★ the cutest kitten ★

Superstar Dreams

Is Chloe brave enough
to perform on stage?

Cuddle uses her
magic to take
Olivia and Grace
backstage at a
talent show. Can
the girls persuade
talented Chloe
to audition even
though she's lost
her lucky charm?

Find out in SUPERSTAR DREAMS...

Cuddle
★ the cutest kitten ★

Princess Party Sleepover

Who wants to be a princess?

Princess Victoria doesn't. She'd much rather be wearing old clothes and climbing trees. Can Cuddle, Olivia and Grace convince her that being a princess can be fun in time for the royal ball?

Find out in PRINCESS PARTY SLEEPOVER...

Puddle
the naughtiest puppy

If you liked Cuddle the Cutest Kitten
you'll love Puddle the Naughtiest Puppy!

Puddle is a mischievous puppy who
appears every time it rains. He only has
to jump into a puddle to take cousins
Ruby and Harry on a series of amazing
magical adventures.

Why not begin your Puddle
collection today?

Learning more about cats

Grace, Olivia and Cuddle have lots of fun on their adventures together, but real cats and kittens need a lot of looking after. That's why our friends at Cats Protection are going to be joining us in each book to talk about everything a cat needs for a happy home life.

Cats are independent but affectionate creatures, and because of this they are one of the most popular pets in Britain, with over 9 million cats being owned. The next page has some interesting facts about our furry friends – did you know any of them already?

Always remember, Cuddle is a magical kitten, while real cats and kittens are living animals who need a lot of care, love and attention.

Did you know?

- A cat can live for over 15 years.
- Cats can see very well in the dark.
- Cats like to sleep for around 16 hours a day.
- Smell is very important to cats: they rub up against people and things to leave their smell on them. This makes them feel safe.
- Cats sweat through their paws.
- Cats can run at speeds of up to 30 miles per hour.
- Microchips give cats a better chance of being found if they go missing: the cat owner's address is stored on the chip and a scanner can reveal who the cat belongs to.

Congratulations – now you know lots of cat facts! We hope you've had fun learning about cats with Cats Protection. See you next time!

Cats Protection is the UK's leading feline welfare charity. Cats Protection has been helping cats since 1927 and each year they help more than 215,000 cats and kittens, giving them the chance of a better life.
To find out more please go to: www.cats.org.uk
For more cool cat facts, games and downloads, visit www.cats.org.uk/cats-for-kids

Spell Scrambles

Look at the strange words below. Can you unscramble each one to make the name of a character from the story? Then match each name to a picture.

1. Smis Dramsuno

2. Mosco

3. Ahl

4. Smosylf

5. Rinsor

A

B

C

D

E

Answers at the back of the book

Cuddle Confusion

Look carefully at the picture of
Cuddle below. Can you work out
which of the images opposite exactly
matches this picture?

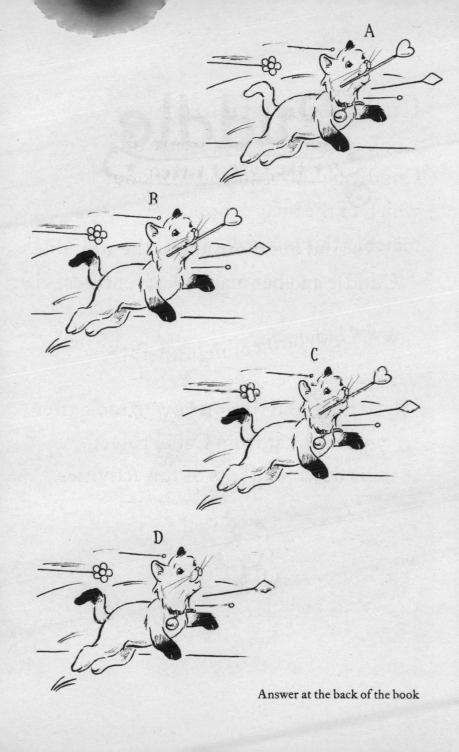

A

B

C

D

Answer at the back of the book

Cuddle
★ the cutest kitten ★

To find out more about the adorable
Cuddle and her magical adventures, visit

www.ladybird.com/cuddlethekitten

Read hints and tips on how to look after
your own cat from Cats Protection,
plus download lots of fun activities.

Find more fantastic Ladybird titles at
www.ladybird.com

Answers to Cuddle Puzzles:
Spell Scrambles: 1: Miss Rosamund – E, 2: Cosmo – A,
3: Hal – D, 4: Mossfly – B, 5: Norris – C.
Cuddle Confusion: C